ELEMENTS OF
LIFE

NITROGEN

NANCY DICKMANN

PowerKiDS
press™

Published in 2019 by **The Rosen Publishing Group, Inc.**
29 East 21st Street, New York, NY 10010

Cataloging-in-Publication Data
Names: Dickmann, Nancy.
Title: Nitrogen / Nancy Dickmann.
Description: New York : PowerKids Press, 2019. | Series: Elements of life | Includes glossary and index.
Identifiers: ISBN 9781538347690 (pbk.) | ISBN 9781538347713 (library bound) | ISBN 9781538347706 (6pack)
Subjects: LCSH: Nitrogen--Juvenile literature. | Group 15 elements--Juvenile literature. | Chemical elements--Juvenile literature.
Classification: LCC QD181.N1 D53 2019 | DDC 546'.711--dc23

For Brown Bear Books Ltd:
Text and Editor: Nancy Dickmann
Designer and Illustrator: Supriya Sahai
Design Manager: Keith Davis
Picture Manager: Sophie Mortimer
Editorial Director: Lindsey Lowe
Children's Publisher: Anne O'Daly

Concept development: Square and Circus/Brown Bear Books Ltd

Picture Credits
Front Cover: Artwork, Supriya Sahai.
Interior: Alamy: Agenja Fotograficzna, 8; iStock: Gannet77, 11t, Kall9, 25, manjik, 10–11, mdesigner124, 16–17, nathan4847, 9, oticki, 20–21, sagarmanis, 24–25, 29b, G Sermek, 17br, 29l, small smiles, 23, Vladimir Vladimirov, 14–15, wxin, 7tr; NASA: JHUAPL, 5; Shutterstock: effective stock photos, 22–23, Gyuszko-Photo, 21t, 28, Val Lawless, 15br, PolakPhoto, 6–7, Andrey Popov, 12.
Key: t=top, b=bottom, c=center, l=left, r=right

Brown Bear Books have made every attempt to contact the copyright holders. If you have any information please contact licensing@brownbearbooks.co.uk

Manufactured in the United States of America

CPSIA Compliance Information: Batch CWPK19: For Further Information contact Rosen Publishing, New York, New York at 1-800-237-9932

CONTENTS

ELEMENTS ALL AROUND US

Have you ever wondered what you're made of? The answer is elements! Everything in the universe is made of elements. These basic substances cannot be broken down into other substances. Carbon, hydrogen, nitrogen, oxygen, phosphorus, and sulfur are the most important to life.

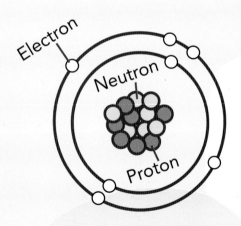

Electron
Neutron
Proton

THE NITROGEN ATOM

A nitrogen atom has 7 electrons and 7 protons. Most nitrogen atoms have 7 neutrons.

IT'S ATOMIC!

Elements are made up of small particles called atoms. Atoms are too small to see, but they are made up of even smaller parts. Atoms of every element contain tiny particles called protons, neutrons, and electrons. Atoms can stick to other atoms in a process called bonding.

NITROGEN EVERYWHERE

Nitrogen is one of the most common elements in the universe. It is formed in stars and is found on some planets and moons. On Earth, it makes up about three-quarters of the atmosphere, and there is nitrogen in every living thing.

There is frozen nitrogen on the surface of the icy dwarf planet Pluto.

Natural or Not?

There are about 94 elements that are found in nature. Others have been made in laboratories.

PHYSICAL PROPERTIES OF NITROGEN

Nitrogen has properties that set it apart from the other elements. Some properties are physical—they can be observed and described fairly easily.

LOOKING AT NITROGEN

You can use your senses to observe some of nitrogen's physical properties. An element's color and odor are both physical properties. Nitrogen is a gas at room temperature, but for solid elements, hardness and shininess are also physical properties. The temperature at which a gas turns into a liquid or freezes solid are physical properties, too.

NIT

RE

STATE: At normal temperature and pressure, nitrogen is a gas. It only turns into a liquid at a very low temperature of −320°F (−196°C).

COLOR: Nitrogen gas has no color, and neither does liquid nitrogen. At extremely low temperatures, nitrogen can freeze into a white solid that looks like snow.

You cannot see or smell the nitrogen in the air that you breathe.

ODOR: Nitrogen has no taste or odor. If it did, you would definitely notice—there is nitrogen in every breath you take.

DENSITY: Nitrogen is not very dense. One liter of nitrogen gas would weigh just 1.25 grams.

CONDUCTIVITY: Nitrogen is not a good conductor of heat or electricity.

Liquid nitrogen must be kept in special tanks to keep it from turning back into a gas.

ROGE

GERATED

IQUID

CHEMICAL PROPERTIES OF NITROGEN

Chemical properties are different from physical properties. These characteristics affect how an element will react with other elements or substances.

CHEMICAL CHANGES

One element can combine with another in a process called a chemical reaction. The atoms are rearranged to form a new substance called a compound. It is during a chemical change like this that scientists can observe an element's chemical properties. These properties include how readily it forms bonds and how easily it burns.

Nitrous oxide is a compound of nitrogen and oxygen. This gas is often given to patients for pain relief.

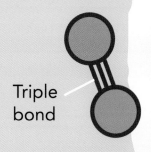
Triple bond

PERFECT PAIR

Two or more atoms bonded together form a molecule. Nitrogen atoms usually join in pairs. They stick together with a very strong bond called a triple bond. A nitrogen atom on its own would react easily with other substances. But once nitrogen atoms pair off, the molecule they form does not react easily.

ALL ABOUT NITROGEN

Here are a few of nitrogen's chemical properties:

At room temperature, nitrogen will not combine with most other elements.

Nitrogen reacts with hydrogen to form a compound called ammonia.

In the presence of lightning or a spark, nitrogen will combine with oxygen to form a compound called nitric oxide.

Ammonia is widely used in fertilizers, which are sprayed on fields.

WHERE IS NITROGEN FOUND?

Nitrogen is one of the most common elements in the universe. It is found in the air, in the ground, and in all living things.

IN THE AIR

You probably know that you breathe in oxygen. But did you know that most of the air you breathe is nitrogen? Molecules of nitrogen together make up about 78 percent of the air on Earth. Just under 21 percent is oxygen. Carbon dioxide and tiny amounts of other gases make up the rest.

Nitrogen is found in the gases from some volcanoes and mineral springs.

Two types of nitrogen–oxygen compounds are produced in the air during electrical storms.

There is nitrogen in the sun and other stars. Saturn's moon Titan has an atmosphere made mostly of nitrogen.

Guano is the solid waste of seabirds and bats. It is rich in nitrogen.

There are nitrogen compounds in many rocks.

There are several different nitrogen compounds in seawater.

HOW NITROGEN WAS DISCOVERED

In the 1770s, Daniel Rutherford trapped a mouse in a sealed container. The mouse soon died from lack of air. Rutherford then burned a candle and a piece of phosphorus in the same air—both reactions use up oxygen. He removed the carbon dioxide from the rest of the gas and was left with nitrogen. He called it "noxious air" because animals couldn't breathe in it.

NITROGEN IN THE BODY

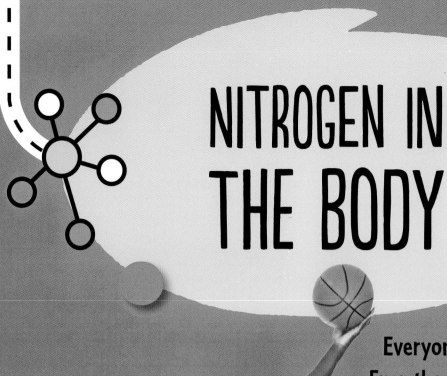

Everyone needs nitrogen. Even though you don't use the nitrogen that you breathe in, your body gets and uses nitrogen in other ways.

THE BIG FOUR

Most of the human body is made up of just four elements: oxygen, carbon, hydrogen, and nitrogen. Nitrogen makes up just over 3 percent of your body's mass. The other three elements make up 93 percent. That leaves less than 4 percent of your body made up of other elements, such as calcium and phosphorus.

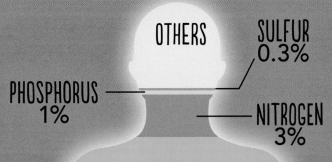

OTHERS

SULFUR
0.3%

PHOSPHORUS
1%

NITROGEN
3%

HYDROGEN
10%

Nitrogen enters your lungs with every breath. Your body cannot absorb nitrogen in the form of a gas, so you breathe it straight out again.

There is nitrogen in amino acids. These molecules join together to form proteins, which help provide structure and do much of the work of the cells.

CARBON
18%

OXYGEN
65%

UNWANTED NITROGEN

Scuba divers carry a mixture of gases in their air tanks, including nitrogen. If a diver comes back to the surface too fast, some of nitrogen forms tiny bubbles in the blood and tissues. This causes a painful condition called "the bends." It can be deadly.

A long, twisting molecule called DNA contains the chemical codes that control traits such as eye color. Nitrogen is an important part of DNA.

BODY BUILDER

Proteins are the most important nitrogen compounds in the human body. They help keep you strong and healthy.

WHAT ARE PROTEINS?

Proteins are large, complicated molecules. There are thousands of different proteins, but they all contain carbon, hydrogen, oxygen, and nitrogen. Proteins are the building materials for the cells that make up the human body. All body parts—from hair and nails to muscles and bones—are made of protein.

Athletes eat plenty of protein to help them build strong muscles.

WHAT PROTEINS DO

Different types of proteins have different roles. Here are just a few of their jobs:

Enzymes are proteins that help start and speed up chemical reactions in the cells.

A protein called hemoglobin, in the blood, transports oxygen to all parts of the body.

Proteins called antibodies protect the body by attaching to harmful viruses and bacteria.

Hormones transmit chemical messages between different parts of the body. Some hormones are proteins.

PROTEINS IN FOOD

Humans take in protein from the food they eat. Meat, fish, and eggs are good sources of protein, and so are milk and dairy products. There is also protein in plant products such as nuts, seeds, tofu, beans, and lentils.

Vegetarians can get all the protein they need from plants.

NITROGEN FIXING

Living things need nitrogen in order to make proteins. To get it, we rely on a process called nitrogen fixation. But why does the element need "fixing"?

UNREACTIVE NITROGEN

Humans and other animals cannot absorb nitrogen from the air. The nitrogen molecules in air do not react easily with other substances. They cannot be used to make compounds, such as proteins. Nitrogen fixation is a way of getting the nitrogen into a form that can be used more easily.

Some nitrogen fixation happens naturally, such as during a thunderstorm.

FIXATION METHODS

Nitrogen can be fixed in three main ways:

The energy in lightning can split nitrogen molecules apart. On their own, the atoms are very reactive. They react with oxygen to form nitrogen oxides. Rain washes these compounds to the ground, where they enter the soil.

Certain bacteria in the soil can convert nitrogen from the air into compounds such as nitrates. There are also nitrogen-fixing bacteria in the roots of legumes such as peas and beans.

In factories, nitrogen can be fixed by mixing it with hydrogen at high temperature and pressure to form ammonia.

Legumes provide sugars for nitrogen-fixing bacteria. In return, they get the nitrogen compounds made by the bacteria.

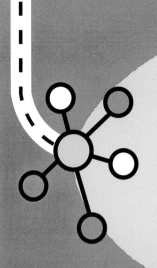

THE NITROGEN CYCLE

We talk about nitrogen being "fixed," but that doesn't mean it stays in one place! Nitrogen atoms circulate around the planet in a process called the nitrogen cycle.

Lightning turns free nitrogen into nitrogen oxides. Rain washes them into the soil.

Animals take in nitrogen when they eat plants.

Tiny decomposers break down animal waste, returning nitrogen to the soil in the form of ammonia.

Chemical Formula

Each compound has a chemical formula that shows how many atoms of each element its molecules contain. Ammonia's chemical symbol is NH_3. This shows that each ammonia molecule has one nitrogen atom and three hydrogen atoms. Nitric oxide is NO (one nitrogen, one oxygen) and nitrogen dioxide is NO_2 (one nitrogen, two oxygen). Nitrogen's chemical formula is N_2 (two nitrogens joined together).

Plants take up nitrogen compounds through their roots. They use them to make proteins.

When fossil fuels are burned, nitrous oxides are released into the air.

Nitrogen is converted to ammonia in factories. The ammonia is used to make fertilizers, which are spread on crops.

Bacteria convert nitrogen from the air into nitrates and other compounds.

Some types of bacteria break down nitrates and return free nitrogen to the air.

FERTILIZER

Farmers depend on fertilizers to help their crops grow bigger and faster. One of the main types of fertilizer puts nitrogen into the soil.

Cereal crops such as wheat take up nitrates from the soil.

GIVE AND TAKE

Plants take nutrients from the soil. If a farmer grows the same crop over and over in the same field, it will use up the nutrients. Farmers must replace the soil's nutrients to keep it healthy. One way to do this is by adding fertilizer.

Natural Fertilizers

Natural fertilizers are rich in nitrogen. Animal manure and guano (the solid waste of seabirds and bats) are both natural fertilizers.

CROP ROTATION

Some crops take nitrates from the soil. Legumes such as peas and beans put nitrogen back into the soil. Their roots are home to nitrogen-fixing bacteria. By planting wheat one year and peas the next, a farmer can keep the soil from running out of nitrogen.

Most modern farmers use nitrogen fertilizers that were made in factories, using ammonia.

THE HABER–BOSCH PROCESS

Nitrogen compounds for making fertilizers used to come from mines, but supplies were running out. Scientists looked for other ways to get the compounds. Fritz Haber found a way to make ammonia. He combined nitrogen from the air with hydrogen at high temperature and pressure. Carl Bosch, worked out how to do this on a massive scale.

POLLUTION

Although nitrogen is a natural substance that all life depends on, it can also be a form of pollution.

FERTILIZER PROBLEMS

Factory-made fertilizers have helped farmers feed the world's growing population. But although they have solved one problem, they are causing another. Rain can wash nitrogen fertilizers off farmland and into rivers and lakes. This starts a process called eutrophication, which can damage the natural environment.

When algae grows rapidly on the water's surface, it is called an algal bloom.

HOW EUTROPHICATION WORKS

Nitrogen compounds in the fertilizer encourage algae to grow. Algae soon covers the water's surface, blocking sunlight from reaching other water plants. The plants die and are broken down by bacteria. These bacteria use up the oxygen in the water, making it hard for animals to survive.

All living things contain nitrogen. Fossil fuels formed from the remains of prehistoric plants and animals.

AIR POLLUTION

Coal, oil, and gas are often called fossil fuels. We use them to power vehicles and factories. When fossil fuels burn, they release nitrogen into the air. This nitrogen can cause smog and acid rain. It can also cause Earth's temperature to rise. Nitrous oxide is a type of greenhouse gas, which traps the sun's heat.

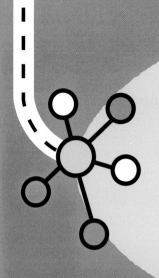

QUICK FREEZE

Nitrogen normally exists as a gas. But when it is frozen into liquid form, it can be very useful—and do amazing things!

SUPER-COLD

Liquid nitrogen is so cold that anything that it touches will freeze instantly. When an object freezes slowly, ice crystals grow and damage the object's structure. Liquid nitrogen freezes things so quickly that the ice crystals stay small and don't cause as much damage.

FLASH FREEZING

Here are just a few of the ways that we use liquid nitrogen:

Liquid nitrogen is used to keep some machines and scientific tools cool.

Scientists use it to freeze and preserve living tissues such as blood or egg cells.

Doctors use it to freeze and remove warts or other skin growths.

It is used to freeze fresh food, such as peas or blueberries, preserving them while keeping their nutrients.

BACK FROM THE DEAD?

Some people have had their entire bodies frozen after they died. They hope that in the future their bodies can be unfrozen and brought back to life. So far, there is no proof that cells will still work again after thawing.

THE PERIODIC TABLE

All the elements are organized into a chart called the periodic table. It groups together elements with similar properties. Each square gives information about a particular element.

A Good Idea!

The periodic table was developed in the 1860s by a Russian chemist named Dmitri Mendeleev. He left gaps that were later filled in with new elements, as they were discovered.

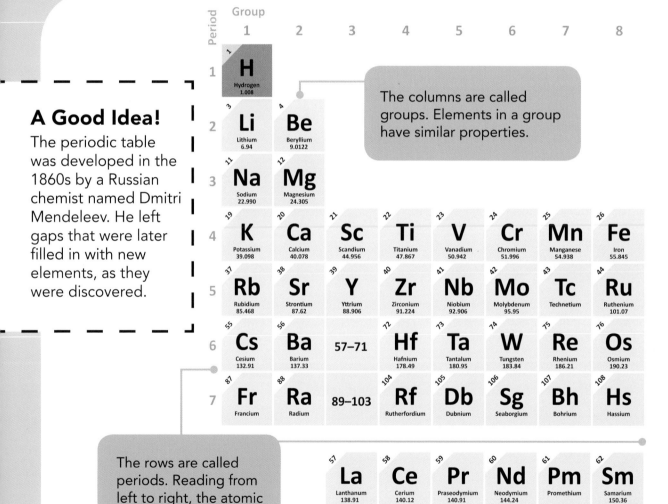

The columns are called groups. Elements in a group have similar properties.

The rows are called periods. Reading from left to right, the atomic numbers of the elements go up, from 1 to 118.

Period	Group 1	2	3	4	5	6	7	8
1	1 **H** Hydrogen 1.008							
2	3 **Li** Lithium 6.94	4 **Be** Beryllium 9.0122						
3	11 **Na** Sodium 22.990	12 **Mg** Magnesium 24.305						
4	19 **K** Potassium 39.098	20 **Ca** Calcium 40.078	21 **Sc** Scandium 44.956	22 **Ti** Titanium 47.867	23 **V** Vanadium 50.942	24 **Cr** Chromium 51.996	25 **Mn** Manganese 54.938	26 **Fe** Iron 55.845
5	37 **Rb** Rubidium 85.468	38 **Sr** Strontium 87.62	39 **Y** Yttrium 88.906	40 **Zr** Zirconium 91.224	41 **Nb** Niobium 92.906	42 **Mo** Molybdenum 95.95	43 **Tc** Technetium	44 **Ru** Ruthenium 101.07
6	55 **Cs** Cesium 132.91	56 **Ba** Barium 137.33	57–71	72 **Hf** Hafnium 178.49	73 **Ta** Tantalum 180.95	74 **W** Tungsten 183.84	75 **Re** Rhenium 186.21	76 **Os** Osmium 190.23
7	87 **Fr** Francium	88 **Ra** Radium	89–103	104 **Rf** Rutherfordium	105 **Db** Dubnium	106 **Sg** Seaborgium	107 **Bh** Bohrium	108 **Hs** Hassium

57 **La** Lanthanum 138.91	58 **Ce** Cerium 140.12	59 **Pr** Praseodymium 140.91	60 **Nd** Neodymium 144.24	61 **Pm** Promethium	62 **Sm** Samarium 150.36
89 **Ac** Actinium	90 **Th** Thorium 232.04	91 **Pa** Protactinium 231.04	92 **U** Uranium 238.03	93 **Np** Neptunium	94 **Pu** Plutonium

Every element has an atomic number. It shows how many protons are in each of its atoms. Nitrogen's atomic number is 7.

The chemical symbol is one or two letters, often an abbreviation of the element's name. It is the same in all languages.

7
N
Nitrogen
14.007

Each square shows the element's name. Different languages use different names.

A number shows the element's atomic weight. It is an average of the number of protons and neutrons in the different isotopes of an element.

9	10	11	12	13	14	15	16	17	18

Metalloids (semimetals)

Non–metals

Metals

| | | | | **5** B Boron 10.81 | **6** C Carbon 12.011 | **7** N Nitrogen 14.007 | **8** O Oxygen 15.999 | **9** F Fluorine 18.998 | **2** He Helium 4.0026 |

| | | | | **13** Al Aluminum 26.982 | **14** Si Silicon 28.085 | **15** P Phosphorus 30.974 | **16** S Sulfur 32.06 | **17** Cl Chlorine 35.45 | **10** Ne Neon 20.180 |

| **27** Co Cobalt 58.933 | **28** Ni Nickel 58.693 | **29** Cu Copper 63.546 | **30** Zn Zinc 65.38 | **31** Ga Gallium 69.723 | **32** Ge Germanium 72.630 | **33** As Arsenic 74.922 | **34** Se Selenium 78.971 | **35** Br Bromine 79.904 | **18** Ar Argon 39.948 |

| **45** Rh Rhodium 102.91 | **46** Pd Palladium 106.42 | **47** Ag Silver 107.87 | **48** Cd Cadmium 112.41 | **49** In Indium 114.82 | **50** Sn Tin 118.71 | **51** Sb Antimony 121.76 | **52** Te Tellurium 127.60 | **53** I Iodine 126.90 | **36** Kr Krypton 83.798 |

| **77** Ir Iridium 192.22 | **78** Pt Platinum 195.08 | **79** Au Gold 196.97 | **80** Hg Mercury 200.59 | **81** Tl Thallium 204.38 | **82** Pb Lead 207.2 | **83** Bi Bismuth 208.98 | **84** Po Polonium | **85** At Astatine | **54** Xe Xenon 131.29 |

| **109** Mt Meitnerium | **110** Ds Darmstadtium | **111** Rg Roentgenium | **112** Cn Copernicium | **113** Nh Nihonium | **114** Fl Flerovium | **115** Mc Moscovium | **116** Lv Livermorium | **117** Ts Tennessine | **86** Rn Radon |

| | | | | | | | | | **118** Og Oganesson |

| **63** Eu Europium 151.96 | **64** Gd Gadolinium 157.25 | **65** Tb Terbium 158.93 | **66** Dy Dysprosium 162.50 | **67** Ho Holmium 164.93 | **68** Er Erbium 167.26 | **69** Tm Thulium 168.93 | **70** Yb Ytterbium 173.05 | **71** Lu Lutetium 174.97 | Lanthanide elements |

| **95** Am Americium | **96** Cm Curium | **97** Bk Berkelium | **98** Cf Californium | **99** Es Einsteinium | **100** Fm Fermium | **101** Md Mendelevium | **102** No Nobelium | **103** Lr Lawrencium | Actinide elements |

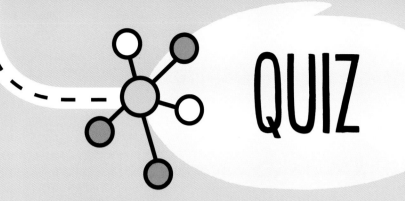

QUIZ

Try this quiz and test your knowledge of nitrogen and elements! The answers are on page 32.

1

What is a proton?

a. one of the particles that makes up an atom
b. a substance made from two different elements
c. a ton that's not an amateur anymore

2

What color is nitrogen?

a. pale pink
b. silvery-blue
c. it has no color

3

Which ingredients make up ammonia?

a. nitrogen and carbon
b. nitrogen and hydrogen
c. eggs, flour, and milk

4

What happens to nitrogen when it enters your lungs?

a. you breathe it straight back out
b. it goes into the bloodstream
c. it gets converted to oxygen

5

Why does nitrogen need to be fixed?

a. because it's broken
b. because otherwise it would just float away
c. so that living things can use it more easily

6

What role do bacteria play in the nitrogen cycle?

a. they convert pure nitrogen into useful compounds
b. they use nitrogen to build proteins
c. comic relief

7

What happens when you dip something in liquid nitrogen?

a. it freezes instantly
b. it becomes invisible
c. it turns into ammonia

8

Why is growing beans good for the soil?

a. they give off more oxygen than other plants
b. they put nitrogen back into the soil
c. they make it smell nice

GLOSSARY

algae tiny plant-like organisms that live in water

amino acid substance that is necessary for building proteins

ammonia strong-smelling compound of nitrogen and hydrogen, which is used to make fertilizer

atmosphere the layers of gases that surround the earth

atom the smallest possible unit of a chemical element

bacteria tiny living things that can cause infection but that can also be useful, such as by breaking down dead matter

bond to form a link with atoms of the same element or of a different element

carbon dioxide gas found in the air that plants need to survive

cell the smallest unit of life. All plants and animals are made of cells.

chemical change change that occurs when one substance reacts with another to form a new substance

chemical property something that is observed during or after a chemical reaction

compound substance made of two or more different elements bonded together

conductor substance that allows heat or electricity to pass through it easily

decomposer living thing, such as a bacterium or insect, that breaks down dead matter

dissolve to mix completely with a liquid

electron a tiny particle of an atom with a negative charge

element a substance that cannot be broken down or separated into other substances

energy the ability to do work. Energy can take many different forms.

fertilizer substance that farmers put on fields to help crops grow better

fossil fuels fuels such as oil, coal, and gas, which are formed from the decaying remains of living things

gas form of matter that is neither liquid or solid

guano the solid waste of seabirds and bats, which can be used as a fertilizer

isotopes different forms of the same element. Isotopes of an element have different numbers of neutrons.

legumes family of plants that grow their seeds and fruits in pods. Beans, peas, and lentils are legumes

liquid form of matter that is neither a solid nor a gas, and flows when it is poured

mass the total amount of matter in an object or space

molecule the smallest unit of a substance that has all the properties of that substance. Molecules are made up of atoms.

neutron a particle in the nucleus of an atom with no electrical charge

physical property characteristic of a material that can be observed without changing the material

proton a positively charged particle in the nucleus of an atom

react to undergo a chemical change when combined with another substance

FURTHER RESOURCES

BOOKS

Amstutz, Lisa J. *Discover Cryobiology.* Minneapolis, MN: Lerner Publications, 2017.

Arbuthnott, Gill. *Your Guide to the Periodic Table.* New York, NY: Crabtree Publishing Company, 2016.

Callery, Sean, and Miranda Smith. *Periodic Table.* New York, NY: Scholastic Nonfiction, 2017.

Carmichael, L.E. *How Can We Reduce Agricultural Pollution?* Minneapolis, MN: Lerner Publications, 2016.

MacCarald, Clara. *Nitrogen.* New York, NY: Enslow Publishing, 2018.

Martin, Bobi. *The Nitrogen Cycle.* New York, NY: Britannica Educational Publishing, 2018.

WEBSITES

Visit this website for information about the nitrogen cycle:
www.ducksters.com/science/ecosystems/nitrogen_cycle.php

Find out more about pollution caused by fertilizer:
www.epa.gov/nutrientpollution/problem

Go here for amazing facts about nitrogen:
www.livescience.com/28726-nitrogen.html

Learn about all the elements using this interactive periodic table:
www.rsc.org/periodic-table/

INDEX

Quiz answers
1. a; 2. c; 3. b; 4. a; 5. c;
6. a; 7. a; 8. b